在威基基海灘(Waikiki)戲水的人群

尼斯(Nice)海岸

唐人街市場(新加坡)

Lifestyles around the World

感恩節的遊行(美國)

康克爾多廣場(法國)

U0084490

製造獨木舟（象牙海岸）

印第安人（美國）

印度教徒

夏天來的聖誕老人（澳大利亞）

市集上的賣花女郎（芬蘭）

尼斯（Nice）的嘉年華會（法國）

大學的畢業典禮（美國）

巴黎（Paris）街上的年輕人
（法國）

戶外烤肉（加拿大）

下午茶時間（英國）

在鬱金香（tulip）田工作的小孩們（荷蘭）

上課中（美國）

美式啦啦隊（美國）

拿波里（Neopolis）的魚市場（義大利）

紐約的街頭（美國）

巴黎的露營場所（法國）

在葡萄園中工作的人們（西德）

LEARNER'S

ALL TALKS 1

LEARNING PUBLISHING CO., LTD.

ALL TALKS

PRINTED IN TAIWAN

supervisor : Samuel Liu
text design : Jessica Y.P. Chen
illustrations : Vivian Wang, Amanda Chang
cover design : Isabella Chang

ACKNOWLEDGEMENTS

We would like to thank all the people whose ongoing support has made this project so enjoyable and rewarding. At the top of the list of those who provided insight, inspiration, and helpful suggestions for revisions are:

David Bell
Pei-ting Lin
Cherry Cheing
Nick Veitch
Joanne Beckett
Thomas Deneau
Stacy Schultz
David M. Quesenberry
Kirk Kofford
Francesca A. Evans
Jeffrey R. Carr
Chris Virani

序　言

　　編者在受教育的過程中，常覺國內的英語教育，欠缺一套好的會話教材。根據我們最近所做的研究顯示，各級學校的英語老師與關心的讀者也都深深覺得，我們用的進口會話教材，版面密密麻麻，不但引不起學習興趣，所學又不盡與實際生活相關。像一般會話書上所教的早餐，總是教外國人吃的 *cereal* （麥片粥），而完全沒有提及中國人早餐吃的稀飯（香港餐館一般翻成＂ *congee* ＂，美國人叫＂ *rice soup* ＂）、豆漿（ *soy bean milk* ）、燒餅（ *baked roll* ）、油條（ *Chinese fritter* 　該如何適切地表達？

　　我們有感於一套好的教材必須能夠真正引發學生的興趣，內容要切合此時此地（ *here and now* ）及讀者確實的需求，也就是要本土化、具體化。

　　五年多來，在這種共識之下，我們全體編輯群秉持專業化的精神，實地蒐集、調查日常生活中天天用得到、聽得到的會話，加以歸類、整理，並設計生動有趣的教學活動，彙編成「ＡＴ美語會話教本」這套最適合中國人的會話教材。

　　這套教材不僅在資料蒐集上力求完美，而且從構思到成書，都投入極大的心力。在編纂期間，特別延聘國內外教學權威，利用這套教材開班授課，由本公司全體編輯當學生，在學習出版門市部親自試用，以求發掘問題，加以修正。因此，這套教材的每一課都經過不斷的實驗改進，每一頁都經過不斷地字斟句酌，輸入中國人的智慧。

　　經由我們的示範教學證明這套教材，祇要徹底弄懂，受過嚴格要求者，英語會話能力定能突飛猛進，短時間內達到高效果。這套教材在編審的每個階段，都務求審慎，唯仍恐有疏失之處，敬祈各界先進不吝指正。

編者　謹識

AT 美語會話教本

課程簡介

AT美語 會話教本	程度	適　用　對　象	備　註
ALL TALKS ①②	初級	1. 具備國中英語程度、初學英會話的讀者。 2. 適合高中、高職、五專的初級英會課程。	已出版
AMERICAN TALKS ①②	中級	1. 具備高中英語程度，以前學過英會的讀者。 2. 適合高中、高職、五專的進階英會課程。 3. 大專程度的初級課程。	已出版
ADVANCED TALKS ①②	高級	1. 想進一步充實流利口語，言之有物的讀者。 2. 大專程度進階用。	已出版

　　全套教材分初、中、高三級；每級二冊，全套共六冊。每冊皆根據教育部頒定的「英語會話課程標準」而設計，每冊十四課。因此可配合各校授課的學年長短，作各種不同的組合利用：

(1) 一學年（兩學期）：採用初級教本 ALL TALKS ①②，內容包括基礎生活會話及一般常見的實用口語，讓同學們學會用最簡單的英語來溝通，打好會話的基礎。

(2) 二學年（四學期）：採用中級教本 AMERICAN TALKS ①② 及高級教本 ADVANCED TALKS ①②。這四冊的內容、人物均可連貫，自成系統。程度由淺入深，舉凡一般簡單的問候、招呼語到基礎商用、談論時事、宗教等會話皆包括在內，涵蓋面廣，可讓同學們循序漸進地培養實力。

(3) 三學年（六學期）：採用全套「AT美語會話教本」六冊，利用一系列設計的整套內容，經由螺旋式教學法，也就是在第一學年教完 ALL TALKS，讓同學們稍具基礎之後，第二、三學年再接著教授 AMERICAN TALKS 及 ADVAN-CED TALKS；一面將前面學過的內容加以整合，一面適度地添加程度與課程，幫助同學們溫故知新，兼顧語言使用的正確性與流暢性。

CONTENTS

CHARACTERS

Lesson 1 Nice to Meet You

**Listen and repeat
after your teacher.**

(A) LET'S TALK

A: Hi, I'm David Lee.
B: Nice to meet you. I'm Angela Lin.

A: Would you like a drink?
B: Yes, please.

A: What do you do, Angela?
B: I work for a newspaper.

A: How do you know Mrs. Brown?
B: We play tennis together. Do you play?

A: No, but I like basketball.
B: How do you know Mrs. Brown?

A: We study English together.
B: Oh.

LESSON 1

🎧 (B) LET'S PRACTICE

Learn the following phrases and do the practice with your partner.

(1) Approach the Person You Are Meeting

1. It's Mr. Brown, isn't it?
2. Excuse me, are you Mr. Thompson?
3. I don't think we've met.
4. What's your name?
5. I don't think I know your name.
6. Hello, I'm Larry.
7. Sorry, I didn't catch your name.

(2) How to Reply

8. Yes, that's right.
9. Yes?
10. Yes, that's right. And you must be Mr. Williams.

(3) How to Introduce Yourself

11. I'm Charles Brown.
12. My name's Sally Brown.
13. May I introduce myself?
14. Please let me introduce myself.

(4) How to Reply to an Introduction

15. How do you do?
16. Hello.

17. (I'm) pleased to meet you.

18. Nice to meet you.

19. Very happy to know you.

20. I've been looking forward to meeting you.

21. So glad to meet you.

PRACTICE 1

Work in pairs. Take turns approaching and introducing yourself to a stranger. Use the following situations:

1. Mr. Peter Brown is meeting Mr. Patrick Lee.
2. Miss Sally Wang is meeting Miss Jane White.
3. Mrs. Fiona Wilson is meeting Mr. William Jones.
4. Mr. David Lee is meeting Miss Jane White.

(5) **Introduce Someone Who Is with You**

22. David, may I introduce Mary?

23. Peter, I'd like you to meet Jennifer.

24. I'd like to introduce my wife.

25. This is my secretary, Jane White.

(6) **To Offer A Drink**

26. Would you like something to drink?

27. Can I get you a drink?

28. What would you like to drink?

29. Would you like a Coke?

(7) To Ask about Someone's Job

30. What do you do?

31. Where do you work?

32. Are you a student?

PRACTICE 2

Work in groups of three. Take turns approaching and introducing yourself to a stranger. Then introduce the person who is with you. Use the following situations:

1. George Blake is meeting Mr. Owen and his business colleague, Jennifer Chen.

2. Charlie Chang introduces himself and his friend Tom to Mary Lee & offers her a drink.

3. You introduce yourself and your wife to David Lee and get to know his profession.

LESSON 1

🎧 (C) LET'S PLAY   ● For Student A

Learn the following sentence patterns first, and ask your partner for the information you need.

How	are	you? your children?
	is	your wife? Jeff?

I'm	
She's He's	fine.
They're	

Where	do you	work?
What	does he	do?

I	am a student. work at a bank.
He's an engineer.	

Is	he she	married?

Yes,	he she	is.	
No,	he she	is	not. divorced. single.

How many	children sons	do you does he	have?

● Ask your partner for information about Deborah Barnett. When you are finished, read the first letters of each word to find out where Deborah is from.

Name: Charles Watson

Occupation: Teacher in an Elementary School.

Marital Status: Married, with one daughter

Hobby: Reading

■ **Charles feels very good today.**

□ Marital Status: _____

□ Occupation: _____

□ Any Children: _____

□ Today's Condition: _____

□ Working Place: _____

□ Hobby: _____

_____

She is from _____

LESSON 1

🎧 (C) LET'S PLAY

● For Student B

Learn the following sentence patterns first, and ask your partner for the information you need.

| How | are | you?
your children? |
| | is | your wife?
Jeff? |

I'm	fine.
She's He's	
They're	

| Where | do you | work? |
| What | does he | do? |

| I | am a student.
work at a bank. |
| He's an engineer. | |

| Is | he
she | married? |

Yes,	he she	is.	
No,	he she	is	not.
			divorced.
			single.

| How many | children
sons | do you
does he | have? |

● Ask your partner for information about Charles Watson. When you are finished, read the first letters of each word to find out where Charles is from.

Name: Deborah Barnett

Occupation: Engineer for Apple Computer Co.

Marital Status: Divorced, with no children

Hobbies: Running and Kung Fu

Deborah was sick yesterday but she is feeling much better today.

☐ Today's Condition: _____

☐ Working Place: _____

☐ Hobby: _____

☐ Marital Status: _____

☐ Number of Children: _____

☐ Any Sons: _____

☐ Occupation: _____

_____

He is from _____

LESSON 1

Exercise

Complete the following dialogue and make your own conversation.

(1) **Dialogue**

A : Hello, My name is _____.

B : Hi. My name is _____.

A : Where are you from?

B : _____. Where are you from?

A : _____.

B : What do you do for a living?

A : I'm a _____, and you?

B : I work _____. What do you do in your free time?

A : I _____. How about you?

B : I _____. Well, I have to go now. Bye.

A : Yes, bye-bye.

(2) **Cartoon**

Lesson 2 See You Next Week

Listen and repeat
after your teacher.

🎧 (A) LET'S TALK

A : Hello, Bill.

B : Hi, Jenny. It's been a long time.

A : Yes. The last time I saw you was in July.

B : I guess it was.

A : How's everything with you?

B : About the same. And you?

A : So-so, I guess.

B : Listen, how would you like to see a movie next Saturday?

A : I'd love to! Give me a call around Thursday or Friday, okay?

B : Okay. Um, I'm running a little late....

A : Me too. Take care, Bill.

B : See you next week.

LESSON 2

(B) LET'S PRACTICE

Learn the following phrases and do the practice with your partner.

(1) Greetings

1. Good morning, Mr. Smith.
2. Good afternoon.
3. Good evening.
4. How are you?
5. I'm fine, thank you.
6. So so.
7. How are you getting along?
8. How are you doing?
9. How's everything?
10. How's life?
11. Is everything all right?
12. What's new?

(2) Long Time No See

13. It's been a long time, hasn't it?
14. I haven't seen you for ages.
15. It's been ages since we last met.
16. Long time no see.
17. How have you been?
18. Have you been well?
19. I'm glad to see you again.

20. It's so nice to see you again.
21. What a coincidence meeting you here !

(3) Bidding Farewell

22. Good-bye.
23. So long, Tom.
24. Good night, Helen.
25. See you tomorrow.
26. See you later.
27. See you around.
28. I'll be seeing you again.
29. I'm glad to have seen you.
30. It's been nice seeing you.
31. It was nice to see you.
32. Nice to have seen you again.

(4) Remembering Others

33. Please say hello to your family.
34. Please remember me to him.
35. Please give my best wishes to her.
36. Please give my love to Jane.
37. Please convey to them my best wishes.
38. My mother asked me to give you her warmest wishes.

PRACTICE 1

Use those phrases you've learned and do the following roleplays.

1. John happens to meet his old friend Tom on the street. They haven't seen each other for 3 years.

2. Jane happens to meet her classmate Judy in front of the drugstore and sends her regards to Judy's mother.

3. Tony happens to meet his friend Mike and asks Mike about his college life.

4. Ms. Wilson happens to meet her neighbor Mr. Jones one morning. They stop to chat.

(5) Leave - Taking

39. I must say good-bye.
40. I must be going.
41. I'd better be on my way.
42. I should be leaving.
43. I have to be getting along now.
44. I'm afraid I should be off now.
45. Well, it's about time to leave, I suppose.
46. I hope you'll also come over to my place.
47. I enjoyed talking to you.
48. I had a very good time.
49. Have a safe trip home.
50. It was nice having you over.

PRACTICE 2

Work in groups of three. Take turns practicing leave-taking in the situations below.

1. Mr. Lee is going to leave Mr. and Mrs. Wilson's party and drive home.

2. Miss White is going to leave the Allens' house and invite them to come to her place sometime.

3. David is going to leave Mrs. Wang's house and thanks her for her delicious meal.

LESSON 2

🎧 (C) LET'S PLAY

● For the Whole Class

Learn the sentence patterns and do the activity together.

Are you	talkative ? married ?
Do you	have a big family ? like dogs ?

Yes, I am. No, I'm not.
Yes, I do. No, I don't.

Were you	born in April ? at home yesterday ?
Did you	watch TV last night ? receive a letter yesterday ?

Yes, I was. No, I wasn't.
Yes, I did. No, I didn't.

● **Find someone in your class who ....**

① _____ likes cats.

② _____ is interested in movies.

③ _____ is married.

④ _____ has three brothers.

⑤ _____ was at home last night.

⑥ _____ was born in July.

⑦ _____ is on a diet.

⑧ _____ needs a new girlfriend.

⑨ _____ wants to see a movie with you.

⑩ _____ is able to cook.

⑪ _____ does not like spicy food.

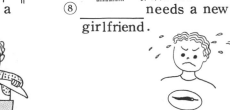

⑫ _____ has an interesting job.

LESSON 2

Exercise

Complete the following dialogue and make your own conversation.

(1) **Dialogue**

A : It's getting late. I'm afraid _____.

B : It was nice _____ you over.

A : I'll be _____ you again.

B : Please _____ to Judy for me.

A : I will. And we'll both be looking _____ to having you over to our house.

B : Have a _____ .

(2) **Cartoon**

Lesson 3 Thank You for Your Help

Listen and repeat after your teacher.

(A) LET'S TALK

A : Excuse me. May I ask you a favor?

B : Of course, if it's anything I can do.

A : Would you be kind enough to take our picture with this camera?

B : Sure.

A : My camera is easy to operate. Just press this button. We'll sit on this bench. ... Is this all right? ... or is this better?

B : That's perfect.

A : Thank you for your help.

B : You are welcome.

LESSON 3

🎧 (B) LET'S PRACTICE

Learn the following phrases and do the practice with your partner.

(1) Asking for Help

1. Please help me.
2. Help me, will you?
3. Give me a hand, please.
4. I wonder if you would help me.
5. May I ask you to help me?
6. Will you please help me?
7. Could you help me?
8. Would you mind helping me?
9. Could you do me a favor?
10. May I ask you a favor?

(2) How to Reply

11. Certainly, I'd be glad to.
12. By all means. What can I do for you?
13. Sure.
14. Okay.
15. Of course, if it's anything I can do.
16. Yes?
17. No problem.
18. What is it?

PRACTICE 1

Role play : Work in pairs. One of you has had car trouble. The other stops to see what happened. Ask for help according to the following information.

1. The car may be running out of gas ; you need a ride to the nearest filling station.

2. The car may have a flat tire ; you need the other's help to change a tire.

3. The car may have engine trouble ; you need the other to call a tow truck for you.

(3) **Thank You**

19. Thank you very much.

20. Thanks a lot.

21. Thanks a million.

22. It's very kind of you.

23. Thank you for your kindness.

24. Thank you for calling.

25. Thank you for the compliments.

26. I appreciate your kindness.

27. Much obliged to you.

28. I'm deeply indebted to you.

29. Thank you for your help.

30. I'm really grateful to you.

31. I don't know how to thank you.

32. Thank you just the same.

(4) **You're Welcome**

33. You're quite welcome.

34. It's my pleasure.

35. The pleasure has been all mine.

36. Not at all. You're welcome.

37. Don't mention it. It's nothing.

38. No trouble at all.

PRACTICE 2

To begin, use expressions like "May I ask you a favor?"

Ask your partner to

1. babysit for you because you have an important appointment tonight.

2. mow your lawn because you're on crutches.

3. give you a hand because your baggage is too heavy.

LESSON 3

🎧 (C) LET'S PLAY   •For Student A

Learn the following sentence patterns first, and ask your partner for the information you need.

Her	hair is	brown. blue.
His	eyes are	black.

He has	a beard. a big nose.
He's got	bushy eyebrows.

Does he	wear glasses ?
	have a moustache ?

Does she	have	a ponytail ? pigtails ? straight or curly hair ?

I think Perhaps Maybe	he	had a long face.
	she	was bald.

● **Play 1**

Help your partner to draw the person below by answering his (her) questions.

Draw your own picture by asking your partner for the information you need.

⇨ Show your drawing to your partner and see which of you is the genius artist.

● **Play 2 —— for the teacher**

"Police artists" can draw pictures of criminals they have never seen, using only the victim's description. Choose someone in the class to be the " police artist " and another class member the criminal. The rest of the class are victims. The artist can get information about the criminal by asking those victims. If the artist can figure out the criminal, then the criminal becomes the new "police artist ".

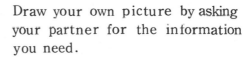

LESSON 3

🎧 (C) **LET'S PRACTICE**　　　　• For Student B

Learn the following sentence patterns first, and ask your partner for the information you need.

Her	hair is	brown.
		blue.
His	eyes are	black.

He has	a beard.
	a big nose.
He's got	bushy eyebrows.

Does he	wear glasses ?
	have a moustache ?

Does she	have	a ponytail ?
		pigtails ?
		straight or
		curly hair ?

I think	he	had a long face.
Perhaps	she	
Maybe		was bald.

● **Play 1**

Help your partner to draw the person below by answering questions.

Draw your own picture by asking your partner for the information you need.

⇨ Show your drawing to your partner and see which of you is the genius artist.

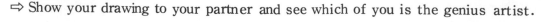

● **Play 2 —— for the teacher**

"Police artists" can draw pictures of criminals they have never seen, using only the victim's description. Choose someone in the class to be the "police artist" and another class member the criminal. The rest of the class are victims. The artist can get information about the criminal by asking those victims. If the artist can figure out the criminal, then the criminal becomes the new "police artist".

LESSON 3

Exercise

Complete the following dialogue and make your own conversation.

(1) **Dialogue**

A : May I ask _____?

B : _____ .

A : Would you be so_____ as to help me _____?

B : No_____ at all. Here you are.

A : Thank you very much.

B : _____ . It was my pleasure.

(2) **Cartoon**

Lesson 4
Would You Please Open the Window?

Listen and repeat after your teacher.

🎧 (A) LET'S TALK

A : Oh, this room is smoky. Somebody must have smoked here. Would you please open the window?

B : Okay. You're right, we need fresh air.

A : That's enough, I think. Thanks.

A : Don't you know where today's paper is?

B : I saw it in the guest-room.

A : Sorry to trouble you, but would you go and fetch it for me?

B : With pleasure. Here it is.

A : Thank you very much.

LESSON 4

(B) LET'S PRACTICE

Learn the following phrases and do the practice with your partner.

(1) How to Make a Request

1. Would you hand me my coat ?
2. Could you give me a ride ?
3. Will you please excuse us for a moment ?
4. I wonder if you'd be willing to babysit for us.
5. Would you mind putting out your cigarette ?
6. Would you please open the window ?

(2) How to Reply

7. Yes, of course.
8. Yes, Certainly.
9. No, not at all.
10. No, of course not.
11. I'm sorry, I can't.
12. I'm sorry I can't, because I already have another commitment that evening.
13. I'm sorry, but it's just not possible.
14. I'm afraid I can't.

PRACTICE 1

Work in pairs. Take turns asking for favors and replying.

1. loan you money (*I'm short of money, too.*)

2. drive you home tonight (*The car is still at the garage.*)

3. help you with your homework (*It's difficult for me, too.*)

4. open the window for you (*I have a cold.*)

Flip a coin to see whether the answer is "Yes" or "No", then reply accordingly. If you can't help your partner, explain why.

(3) Ask Permission

15. May I use your phone?

16. Can I sit here?

17. Could I borrow your lawnmower?

18. I wonder if I could discuss this with you in person.

19. Is it all right if I smoke?

20. Do you mind if I switch the channel?

(4) Offer to Do Something

21. Shall I wake you up?

22. Do you want me to mail the letter for you?

23. Would you like me to meet you at the airport?

(5) How to Reply

24. Yes, please. Thank you.

25. That's very kind of you.

26. No, thanks. I can manage.

27. No, there is no need. Thanks just the same.

28. No, that's all right, thank you.

PRACTICE 2

Work in pairs. Take turns making and accepting offers, using the pictures and words below.

1. help you move the piano

2. close the window

3. drive you to work

4. turn on the airconditioner

5. buy you a hamburger

6. mail this package for you

LESSON 4

🎧 (C) LET'S PLAY   • For Student A

Learn the following sentence patterns first, and ask your partner for the information you need.

May Could	I	borrow use	your car ?
			this pen ?

I need it to	take my girlfriend out.
	write a letter.

By all means.
Help yourself.

I'm sorry, but	I've already lent it to someone else.
	I'll be using it myself.
	I don't like to lend it out.

Thanks anyway.

• Think of another three things which you don't usually lend out. Write them in the boxes below:

Yes / No	Yes / No	Yes / No	Yes / No	Yes / No

• Now ask your partner to lend you these items. Explain why you need to borrow them. How many times did your partner say yes?

⇨ What would your partner like to borrow? For what reason?

Yes / No	Yes / No	Yes / No	Yes / No	Yes / No

LESSON 4

(C) LET'S PLAY

• For Student B

Learn the following sentence patterns first, and ask your partner for the information you need.

May Could	I	borrow use	your car? this pen?

I need it to	take my girlfriend out. write a letter.

By all means.
Help yourself.

I'm sorry, but	I've already lent it to someone else. I'll be using it myself. I don't like to lend it out.

Thanks anyway.

• Think of another three things which you don't usually lend out. Write them in the boxes below:

Yes / No	Yes / No	Yes / No	Yes / No	Yes / No

• Now ask your partner to lend you these items. Explain why you need to borrow them. How many times did your partner say yes?

➡ What would your partner like to borrow? For what reason?

Yes / No	Yes / No	Yes / No	Yes / No	Yes / No

LESSON 4

Exercise

Complete the following dialogue and make your own conversation.

(1) Dialogue

A : Hi, Jane, _____ buy 3 stamps for me, please ?

B : Yes, _____ . And _____ mail this letter, too ?

A : Yes, please. By the way, _____ lend me the typewriter tonight ?

B : _____ . I have to type my midterm papers tonight.

A : I see.

(2) Cartoon

① Would you _____ if I borrowed your car ?

② Well, when exactly ?

③ Until Thursday of next week.

④ I'm sorry, but _____ .

Lesson 5 How about a Game of Tennis?

**Listen and repeat
after your teacher.**

(A) LET'S TALK

A: Let's get together sometime, what do you say?
B: Okay. What did you have in mind?

A: Are you free tomorrow afternoon?
B: Yes, I think so.

A: Then how about a game of tennis?
B: Sounds great. At what time?

A: Is two o'clock too early?
B: No, two's fine. Shall I pick you up at your house?

A: It might be better if we met at the gym.
B: All right, then, let's do that.

LESSON 5

🎧 (B) LET'S PRACTICE

Learn the following phrases and do the practice with your partner.

(1) **Asking for a Suggestion**

  1. What shall we do tonight?

  2. What would you like to eat tonight?

  3. When would you like to visit her?

  4. What can we do over the week-end?

  5. Who do you suggest we invite to the party?

(2) **Making Suggestions**

  6. How about playing tennis with me?

  7. What about going for a drive?

  8. Would you like a drink?

  9. How would you like to get started right away?

10. Why don't you come in and wait inside here?

11. What do you say we go into town for dinner?

12. Would you care for another drink?

13. What do you say to going now?

14. Let's take a walk.

15. Shall we take a walk?

16. Let's take a walk, shall we?

17. Won't you take a walk?

18. Would you like to take a walk?

19. Can we take a walk?

20. I suggest we go and see her tomorrow.

21. Why not go to the pub?

PRACTICE 1

Work in pairs. A asks for a suggestion. B looks at the pictures and makes a suggestion.

1. on Sunday

2. tomorrow

3. tonight

4. over the
    week-end

5. during sum-
    mer vacation

6. tomorrow
    night

(3) Accepting a Suggestion

22. Yes, good idea.

23. Yes, that would be nice.

24. Yes, that seems all right.

25. Yes, that's a great idea.

(4) **Rejecting a Suggestion**

26. No, I can't.

27. No, I don't think so.

28. Well, I'd rather not, if you don't mind.

29. Well, I'm not sure. I don't really feel like it.

PRACTICE 2

Work in pairs. Take turns accepting and rejecting the suggestions below.

1. Let's go for a walk.

2. How about having a party on Sunday?

3. Why don't we try Chinese food tonight?

4. Shall we go now?

5. Would you like to watch TV with me tonight?

LESSON 5

(C) LET'S PLAY

● For Student A

Learn the following sentence patterns first, and ask your partner for the information you need.

How about	going to a movie tonight?
Would you like to	take a walk? come with me?

Well,	that's a good idea,	but there aren't any good film on tonight.
	I'd rather watch TV at home,	if you don't mind.
		if that's all right with you.

I wish I could, but	I have an exam tomorrow.
	I must go shopping now.

● **Read your role card, then begin.**

1. You are calling Jenny, your classmate, to go out tonight. You are looking at the classified ads and making suggestions.

2. Your girlfriend is calling you to discuss what to do tomorrow, since tomorrow is Sunday. But you want to do something else. Try to reject her suggestion and make a counter-suggestion.

🎧 (C) LET'S PLAY

• For Student B

Learn the following sentence patterns first, and ask your partner for the information you need.

How about	going to a movie tonight?
Would you like to	take a walk? come with me?

Well,	that's a good idea,	but there aren't any good film on tonight.
	I'd rather watch TV at home,	if you don't mind.
		if that's all right with you.

I wish I could, but	I have an exam tomorrow.
	I must go shopping now.

• **Read your role card, then begin.**

1. Your classmate, Tom, is calling you to kill time together, but you don't want to. Try to reject his suggestions without hurting his feelings.

2. You are calling your boyfriend to make suggestions about how to spend Sunday together. Use the suggestions below.

LESSON 5

Exercise

Complete the following dialogue and make your own conversation.

(1) **Dialogue**

A : _____ you like a drink?
B : Thanks! _____ you sit down?

A : Would you _____ for another one?
B : No , thanks. _____ do you ____ we go for a drive?

A : Sure, _____ go to my place.
B : It _____ be _____ if we went somewhere else.

(B) **Cartoon**

Lesson 6 I Beg Your Pardon?

**Listen and repeat
after your teacher.**

(A) LET'S TALK

A : Excuse me, but is that Professor Smith's office?
B : Huh? I beg your pardon?

A : Which way to Professor Smith's office?
B : Could you repeat that one more time?

A : I'm looking for Professor Smith!
B : Oh, that's what I thought you said.

A : I don't follow you. What are you driving at?
B : Sorry — you see, I'm Professor Smith.

A : I beg your pardon!
B : That's quite all right.

LESSON 6

(B) LET'S PRACTICE

Learn the following phrases and do the practice with your partner.

(1) **I Didn't Hear You**

1. I'm sorry I didn't catch what you said.
2. I couldn't get what you said.
3. I didn't catch you.
4. I can't hear you very well.
5. I'm sorry, I don't understand you.

(2) **What Did You Say?**

6. I beg your pardon?
7. Would you mind repeating what you said?
8. Could you say it again?
9. May I ask you to say that once more?
10. Would you mind repeating that, please?
11. Would you repeat that again, please?
12. Could you possibly repeat that one more time?
13. What did you say?
14. What was that again?
15. What's your name again, please?
16. Will you please speak a little more slowly?
17. Would you please speak a little louder?

(3) **What Do You Mean?**

18. What do you mean by that?

19. What are you driving at?
20. Do you follow me?
21. Do you get me now?
22. Isn't my meaning clear?
23. Do you mean that I have to go now?

PRACTICE 1

Help the clerk of MacDonald's ask these hard-to-understand customers to repeat what they just said so that the clerk can follow it.

1.

2. I ... I wwant ...ta...hham... bbegger tto go...

3. Give me ~~~~~~ !

4.

5. I want a Colonel hamburger!

* MacDonald's doesn't serve "Colonel hamburger."

(4) **Now I Understand**

24. Oh, there it is.
25. I see.
26. I know.
27. I got it.

28. I understand.
29. Is that so?
30. Is that right?
31. Really?

PRACTICE 2

Work in pairs. Pick a topic that one of you knows about but the other doesn't. The "expert" should explain the topic so that the other person can understand it. The non-expert should ask for clarification where necessary. Then switch roles.

Ideas for topics:

Novels   Sports   Hobbies

Cooking   Stocks   Cars

❖ A warming-up for (C) LET'S PLAY — uncountable nouns

some milk   some coffee   some cake   some sugar
a *bottle* of milk   a *jar* of coffee   a *piece* of cake   a *packet* of sugar

some water   some juice   some bread   some lettuce
a *glass* of water   a *carton* of juice   a *loaf* of bread   a *head* of lettuce

LESSON 6

🎧 (C) **LET'S PLAY**   ● For Student A

Learn the following sentence patterns first, and ask your partner for the information you need.

What've	you / they	got in that bag?		I've / We've / They've	got	a pair of gloves. / a packet of tea. / some sugar. / two books.
What's	he / she			He's / She's		

Have you	got	a pair of gloves? / two books? / some sugar?		Yes,	I have. / he has.
Has he				No,	I haven't. / he hasn't.

● Ask your partner if he (she) has the things below. If yes, put a check mark on that item.

● Here are the things you've got.

● Ask your partner what he (she) has in the basket. And draw in the items accordingly.

● Here are the things in your suit-case.

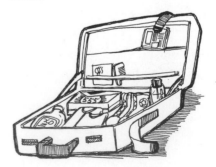

LESSON 6

♥ (C) LET'S PLAY

• For Student B

Learn the following sentence patterns first, and ask your partner for the information you need.

What've	you they	got in that bag?
What's	he she	

Have you	got	a pair of gloves? two books? some sugar?
Has he		

I've We've They've	got	a pair of gloves. a packet of tea. some sugar. two books.
He's She's		

Yes,	I have.
	he has.
No,	I haven't.
	he hasn't.

• Here are the things you've got.

• Here are the things in your basket.

• Ask your partner if he(she) has the things below. If yes, put a check mark on that item.

• Ask your partner what he(she) has in the suitcase. And draw in the items accordingly.

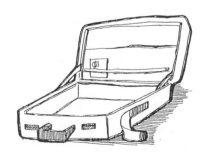

LESSON 6

Exercise

Complete the following dialogue and make your own conversation.

(1) Dialogue

A : I think George may have had a little help on last week's test. Do you _____ me?

B : No. What do you _____ by that?

A : Isn't my meaning clear? He made an A, even though he didn't study.

B : What are you _____ at? Do you _____ to say that he might have been cheating?

A : Uh-huh.

B : Oh! Now _____.

(2) Cartoon

Lesson 7 Congratulations!

**Listen and repeat
after your teacher.**

(A) LET'S TALK

A : You look very sharp in your graduation robes.
B : Thanks, Uncle Bob.

A : Congratulations. I'm real proud of you.
B : That's very nice of you.

A : Are you looking forward to your new job?
B : Yeah, I guess so.

A : Well, I'm sure you'll be a success.
B : I've been applying to graduate schools, Uncle Bob.

A : Great! I always knew you were a scholar.
B : I hope you're right.

LESSON 7

(B) LET'S PRACTICE

Learn the following phrases and do the practice with your partner.

(1) Compliments

1. You're looking very well, as usual.
2. You look very fit.
3. You look very nice in your new dress.
4. You certainly have a wonderful taste in clothes.
5. You've got a good sense of humor.
6. That suit is very becoming to you.
7. That's a nice suit you're wearing.
8. That tie matches your coat well.
9. That tie goes very well with your coat.
10. You look wonderful with that hairdo.
11. You always seem to be in tip-top condition.
12. You have a good memory!
13. You're fantastic!
14. You sure do write good essays.

(2) Replies

15. Thank you.
16. Thank you for the compliment.
17. You look nice, too.

PRACTICE 1

Work in pairs. Take turns making and responding to compliments in the following situations.

1. You are wearing a new dress today.
2. You just had your hair cut yesterday.
3. You just finished reciting a long poem by Robert Frost.
4. Your friend, Jim Wilson, can use chopsticks very well.

(3) Congratulations

18. Congratulations!
19. Congratulations on your promotion!
20. Let me congratulate you on passing the exam.
21. Congratulations! I knew you'd succeed.
22. Let me offer my hearty congratulations.
23. Congratulations on your graduation!
24. Congratulations on your wedding!

(4) Replies

25. Thank you.
26. I guess I was just lucky.
27. Thank you. I hope to see you at our wedding reception!

PRACTICE 2

Work in pairs. Take turns playing roles suggested by the situations below.

1. graduate

2. get married

3. have a baby

4. get promoted

(5) Special Occasions

28. Merry Christmas!

29. Happy New Year!

30. Happy Easter!

31. Happy Thanksgiving Day!

32. Many happy returns of the day!

33. Happy Birthday!

34. Happy golden anniversary!

(6) Replies

35. Thank you.

36. The same to you!

PRACTICE 3

Work in pairs. Greet each other with an appropriate phrase for the following holidays!

LESSON 7

🎧 (C) LET'S PLAY

• For the Whole Class

Learn the following sentence patterns, then do the activity.

Is it some kind of	animal?
	fruit?
	building?
	tool?

Is it	in the ocean?
	expensive?
	in the city?
	useful?

Can we	use it to write?
	eat it?
	find it in our classroom?

• **"Charades" is a guessing game. The object is to communicate without speaking. Here are directions for the teacher:**

① Draw a slip of paper with a word written on it.

② Read your word. Don't let anybody else see it.

③ Now act out that word without speaking, while the rest of the class makes guesses.

④ If someone comes close, point to them. Make a circle in the air with your finger. This means "keeping going."

⑤ When some-one guesses your word, then you're finished.

⑥ Divide the class into two groups. The group guessing out the more answers within a limited time wins!

Who wins?

LESSON 7

🎧 (D) LET'S LOOK

● Work in Pairs

What's going on here? And what will probably happen next? Work in pairs. Think of a story for each window.

There are	three people two boys one man and one woman	in the window.
There is one person		in the room.

She He	is	reading the newspaper. playing the piano.
They	are	playing cards.
I	am	lifting weights.

I They	try		practice hard	because	I they	have a performance tomorrow.
The father tries		to	interrupt the proposal		he	doesn't like his daughter's boyfriend.

● Compare your stories with your partner and think of a story for yourself.

LESSON 7

Exercise

Complete the following dialogue and make your own conversation.

(1) Dialogue

A : _____.
B : Thanks! So do you.

A : _____.
B : Thanks! My mother gave it to me.

A : Jane and I are getting married.
B : _____!

A : Congratulations on winning the election!
B : Thanks! I'll _____.

(2) Cartoon

① _____ winning the essay contest!

② Thank you, John.

③ You ____ ___ write good essays.

④ I love to write, but I was ____, too.

Lesson 8 I'm Sorry for Being Late

Listen and repeat after your teacher.

(A) LET'S TALK

A : Oh, I'm sorry for being late. Have I kept you waiting long?

B : No, you haven't. I also came just a minute ago.

A : I'm glad to hear that. The traffic was so heavy.

B : Yes, I know. It's particularly bad at this time of day.

A : Next time I'll be sure to leave earlier.

B : Don't worry about it. If could happen to anyone.

A : Thanks for being so understanding.

LESSON 8

🎧 (B) LET'S PRACTICE

Learn the following phrases and do the practice with your partner.

(1) Apologizing

1. I am very sorry.
2. I'm awfully sorry.
3. I'm sorry to have kept you waiting long.
4. I beg your pardon.
5. I'm sorry for what I've done.
6. It was my fault.
7. I am to blame.
8. I really didn't mean that.
9. Please forgive me.
10. It was most thoughtless of me.
11. I didn't mean to hurt your feelings.
12. Please accept my sincere apology.
13. I really didn't mean to do it.

(2) Accepting Apologies

14. That's all right.
15. Don't mention it. It doesn't matter.
16. Don't worry about it.
17. Never mind. Forget it.
18. Please don't apologize. You haven't hurt me at all.
19. Please don't worry about it.
20. It's me that should apologize.
21. Oh, it doesn't matter.

PRACTICE 1

Work in pairs. Practice apologizing and accepting apologies using the following situations.

1. You are late for a job interview because your alarm clock didn't go off.

2. It's your turn to do the laundry, and you ruin your roommate's nice shirt.

3. You forget to pay the rent on time.

4. You have lost the book which you borrowed from your classmate, John.

5. You are late for class again and the teacher is very angry.

6. You promised your girlfriend that you would go to the movies with her after work. But you were asked to work overtime.

(3) **Expressing Sympathy**

22.　I'm very sorry to hear of your misfortune.

23.　Please accept my deepest sympathy.

24.　I offer my deepest condolences.

25. Please extend my deepest condolences to your family.

26. I was deeply shocked to hear of the loss of your father.

27. I don't know what to say.

28. I'm sorry to hear of your bereavement.

29. I don't have adequate words to express my sympathy.

(4) Words of Comfort

30. I can well understand your feelings.

31. Please don't be too discouraged.

32. Cheer up!

33. Take it easy. You can make it.

34. Hang in there!

35. Don't give up.

PRACTICE 2

Work in pairs. Take turns expressing sympathy and words of comfort according to the situations below.

1. Your friend Jane's father just died yesterday. You are calling to express your sympathy.

2. Your classmate, Julie, just failed the mid-term exam. Say something to comfort her.

3. Your friend, David, was fired by his boss. Say something to cheer him up.

4. Your younger brother is nervous about the speech contest tomorrow. Say something to encourage him.

LESSON 8

(C) LET'S PLAY

• For Student A

Learn the following sentence patterns first, and ask your partner for the information you need.

Could Can May	we cook in the dorm? I take a dog to the Twin Pines Mall?

Yes, that's Yes, it's	all right.

Is it	all right ok	to smoke?

No,	you	can't. shouldn't.

Is	drinking	allowed in the dorm?
Are	beggars pets	permitted in the mall?

No,	It's they're	not allowed. against the rules.

• **Work in pairs. One of you read this page, while the other reads the next page. Talk about picture A without looking at your partner's page. Decide whether any rules are being broken.**

A

• **How many rules are being broken?**

LESSON 8

(C) LET'S PLAY

• For Student B

Learn the following sentence patterns first, and ask your partner for the information you need.

Could Can May	we cook in the dorm? I take a dog to the Twin Pines Mall?		Yes, that's Yes, it's	all right.	
Is it	all right ok	to smoke?	No,	you	can't. shouldn't.
Is Are	drinking beggars pets	allowed in the dorm? permitted in the mall?	No,	it's they're	not allowed. against the rules.

• Work in pairs. One of you read this page, while the other reads the previous page. Talk about picture A without looking at your partner's page. Decide whether any rules are being broken.

A

B

Student Handbook p.6

Dorm Rules and Regulations
1. No cooking in dorm rooms.
2. No fire or open flame.
3. No stereo playing after midnight.
4. No pets (except fish).
5. No alchoholic **beverages**.
6. No illegal drugs.
7. Visiting hours from
   8:00 pm—12:00 pm weekdays
   11:00pm— 1:00pm weekends

• **How many rules are being broken?**

LESSON 8

Exercise

Complete the following dialogue and make your own conversation.

(1) **Dialogue**

A : My husband died last week.

B : I'm _____ to hear of your _____. Please accept
my _____.

A : It was such a shock.

B : I can understand _____. But _____ in there.

A : I just can't go on any more without Joe.

B : I don't know what to _____. If there's _____ I can
do, please ask.

(2) **Cartoon**

Lesson 9

That's Great!

Listen and repeat
after your teacher.

🎧 (A) LET'S TALK

A : Happy birthday, Emily.
B : Thank you!

A : Here's a little something for you.
B : Oh, thank you very much! May I open it now?

A : Sure, go right ahead.
B : Oh, what a lovely blouse! Thank you!

A : I hope it's the right size.
B : Wait a moment while I try it on.

A : Hey! It fits exactly!
B : That's great!

LESSON 9

(B) LET'S PRACTICE

Learn the following phrases and do the practice with your partner.

(1) **Joy**

  1. Oh wow!

  2. Wonderful.

  3. Splendid.

  4. Excellent.

  5. Incredible.

  6. That's fine.

  7. That's great.

  8. I'm so glad.

  9. Hurrah! Hurray!

10. How lucky!

11. That's nice.

12. Thank God.

(2) **Sadness**

13. Good Lord.

14. I'm so sad!

15. How sad I am!

16. Oh my God!

17. Oh dear.

18. How awful!

19. My!

20. Oh no.

21. How unlucky!

22. That's too bad!

23. What a pity!

(3) **Shock and Anger**

24. You idiot!

25. Aren't you ashamed?

26. Shame on you!

27. How dare you say such a thing?

28. What a shame!

29. You ought to be ashamed of yourself.

30. I'm fed up with it!

31. You've done what?

32. Oh, how could you do that?

33. Darn it!

34. I just can't believe it.

(4) **Apathy and Disbelief**

35. Nonsense!

36. You must be kidding.

37. Are you serious?

38. You can't be serious.

39. I wouldn't be surprised.

40. Who cares?

PRACTICE 1

Work in pairs. Take turns breaking the following pieces of news, as well as any others you think of. React to that situation appropriately.

1. Your dog died.

2. You just won one million dollars.

5. Your sister posed for a men's magazine.

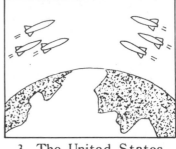

3. The United States and Soviet Union are at war.

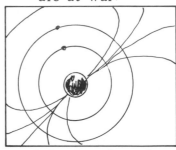

6. Scientists have just discovered a second moon of Pluto.

4. Your son made straight A's on his report card.

7. Your job has been taken over by a computer.

LESSON 9

(C) LET'S PLAY
•For Student A

Learn the following sentence patterns first, and ask your partner for the information you need.

Do you	think	that	UFO'S exist?
Don't you	believe		computers can think?
	imagine		there will be another war?

Maybe	that's true.
Perhaps	computers will become obsolete.
It could be that	world leaders will all sign peace treaties.

| It's | impossible | for | whales | to | talk. |
| | difficult | | people | | survive a nuclear war. |

I	really don't	agree.
		think so.
		know.
	can't tell.	

• **Work in pairs. Talk about the future. Ask your partner whether he(she) thinks any of these things will happen.**

UFO's will reveal themselves to the world.

After a nuclear war, survivors will live like animals.

Computers will enslave people.

People will live on other planets.

LESSON 9

🎧 (C) LET'S PLAY

● For Student B

Learn the following sentence patterns first, and ask your partner for the information you need.

Do you Don't you	think believe imagine	that	UFO'S exist ? computers can think? there will be another war?

Maybe Perhaps It could be that	that's true. computers will become obsolete. world leaders will all sign peace treaties.

It's	impossible difficult	for	whales people	to	talk. survive a nuclear war.

I	really don't	agree. think so. know.
	can't tell.	

● **Work in pairs. Talk about the future. Ask your partner whether he(she) thinks any of these things will happen.**

Humans will live in domed cities to protect themselves from pollution.

Many teachers will lose their jobs because children will study through TV.

Scientists will learn to talk with whales.

There will be peace on earth.

LESSON 9

Exercise

Complete the following dialogue and make your own conversation.

(1) **Dialogue**

A : Mom, Dad, I was offered a scholarship to Harvard.

B : That's _____ ! I'm so _____ of you.

A : But I'm not going.

B : Oh, ___! Why not?

A : I'm marrying my boyfriend instead.

B : You can't be _____ . I just can't_____.

A : You see, we have to get married.

B : _____ on you! I'm ___ up with this _____ .

(2) **Cartoon**

Lesson 10 I'll Have a Steak

Listen and repeat
after your teacher.

(A) LET'S TALK

A : A table for one, please.

B : Right this way, sir.

      *   *   *

B : Are you ready to order ?

A : Yes, I believe I'll have a steak like that lady's having.

B : And how would you like that cooked ?

A : Medium rare. Do I get a salad with that ?

B : You have your choice of a tossed salad or a baked potato.

A : A tossed salad sounds good.

B : And what would you like to drink ?

A : I'll have a martini.

B : Very good, sir. Enjoy your meal !

LESSON 10

🎧 (B) LET'S PRACTICE

Learn the following phrases and do the practice with your partner.

(1) Advance Arrangements

1. I want to make a reservation for three for 7 o'clock.
2. Can we have a table by the window, please?
3. A table for two, please.
4. Do you have a table for four?
5. Sorry, the tables are all occupied now.
6. Could you wait at the bar please?
7. How long do I have to wait?

(2) Ordering

8. Do you have a vegetarian menu?
9. May I take your order?
10. What do you recommend?
11. I've not decided yet.
12. I'd like to order, please.
13. I'll have this.
14. I'll have the same.
15. What would you like to drink?
16. Are you ready to order?

PRACTICE 1

Work in pairs. One of you is the waiter; the other is the customer in a restaurant.

1. You want a table by the window and a vegetarian menu.

2. The waiter is ready to take the order, but you haven't decided yet. You want to ask the waiter for his suggestion.

3. The seats are all taken up. You want to know how long you have to wait.

(3) **Special Foods**

17. Will you show me the wine list?

18. May I order wine by the glass?

19. How would you like your egg?

20. An omelette, please.

21. Scrambled eggs, please.

22. Hard-boiled eggs, please.

23. I'll have fried eggs sunny-side up.

24. I'll have fried eggs, over easy.

25. How would you like your steak?

26. I'd like my steak rare, please.

27. Medium rare, please.

28. Medium, please.

29. Well-done, please.

30. How would you like your coffee?

31. With sugar and cream, please.

32. I take my coffee black.

(4) **Paying Up**

33. Check, please!

Western	Chinese
raw	1～2分熟
rare	3分熟
medium-rare	4分熟
medium	5 分熟
medium-well	6～7分熟
well-done	8～10分熟

34. Let's go Dutch.

35. How much is my share?

36. Give us separate checks, please.

37. Is the service charge included in the bill?

38. It's on me.

39. You shortchanged me.

40. There must be a mistake on the bill.

PRACTICE 2

Work in pairs. One is the waiter; the other is the customer. Practice ordering the foods illustrated below. Then switch roles.

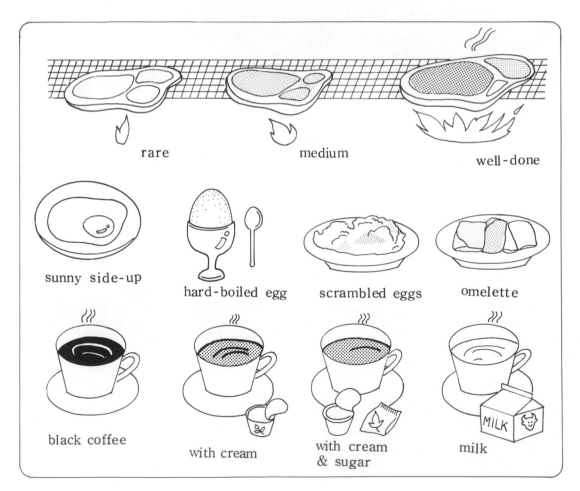

rare   medium

well-done

sunny side-up

hard-boiled egg   scrambled eggs   omelette

black coffee

with cream

with cream
& sugar

milk

LESSON 10

(C) LET'S PLAY

• For Student A

Learn the following sentence patterns first, and ask your partner for the information you need.

Are you ready to Would you like to What would you like to	order ?

I'll have	a steak.
I'd like	French fries.

How would you like your	steak?
	egg ?

What kind of	dressing	would you like ?
	dessert	

Well done,	please.
Sunny-side up,	

I'll take	Russian.
	apple pie.

Would you	like	something to drink?
	care for	anything else ?

Yes, please.
Not yet, thanks. I'm afraid we don't.

COUNTRY KITCHEN

Breakfast Menu

Pancakes	$ 0.99
Waffles	$ 0.99
Toast	$ 0.75
Buttered rolls	$ 0.80
* * *	
Fried eggs	$ 1.50
Scrambled eggs	$ 1.50
Poached eggs	$ 1.50
Boiled eggs	$ 1.50
Omelette	$ 1.50
* * *	
Sausage links	$ 1.00
Ham	$ 1.00
Bacon	$ 1.50
* * *	

Cold cereal	$ 0.50
Hot oatmeal	$ 0.50
* * *	
Coffee	$ 1.75
Tea	$ 1.75
Milk	$ 1.75
Orange juice	$ 1.75
Tomato juice	$ 1.75

• Order what you want for breakfast. Remember you only have 5 dollars. Your partner will take your order. After the meal, go to the counter to pay your bill.

Skyline *Restaurant*		
1		
2		
3		
4		
5		
6		
total	$	
THANK YOU	No 1452	

• Now, you are the waiter (waitress). Write down what your customer orders and get the total amount.

LESSON 10

🎧 (C) LET'S PLAY

• For Student B

Learn the following sentence patterns first, and ask your partner for the information you need.

Are you ready to Would you like to What would you like to	order ?

I'll have I'd like	a steak. French fries.

How would you like your	steak ? egg ?

Well done, Sunny-side up,	please.

What kind of	dressing dessert	would you like?

I'll take	Russian. apple pie.

Would you	like care for	something to drink ? anything else ?

Yes, please.
Not yet, thanks. I'm afraid we don't.

Skyline Restaurant

Soup			
Chicken noodle soup	$1.75	Cheeseburger	$0.75
Beef broth	$1.50	Steak sandwich	$3.00
Tomato soup	$1.50	**Main Dishes**	
Split pea soup	$1.50	Veal	$1.75
Seafood		Roast beef	$5.00
		Chicken breast	$3.50
Shrimp	$2.50	Pork chops	$4.75
Grilled fish	$4.00	Sirloin steak	$5.75
Boiled lobster	$5.00	**Drinks**	
Vegetables		Coffee	$1.75
Baked potato	$0.75	Tea	$0.75
French fries	$0.75	Milk	$0.30
Green beans	$0.75	Orange juice	$0.10
Carrots	$0.75	7-up	$0.50
Peas	$0.75		
Brocolli	$0.75	**Dessert**	
Green salad	$0.75	Ice cream	$0.60
Sandwiches		Cake	$0.50
Bacon, lettuce & Tomato	$1.50	Apple pie	$1.25
Hero	$2.00	Pudding	$1.25
Hamburger	$0.99		

• Look at this menu. Order your lunch. Remember you only have 10 dollars. Your partner will take your order. After the meal, go to the counter to pay your bill.

COUNTRY KITCHEN

No 18

1		
2		
3		
4		
5		
6		
total	$	

• Now, you are the waiter (waitress). Write down what your customer orders and get the total amount.

LESSON 10

Exercise

Complete the following dialogue and make your own conversation.

(1) **Dialogue**

A : A _____ for two, please. We have _____ .

B : Right this _____, please. May I take your _____ ?

A : I'll _____ the lobster salad.

B : And you, madam ?

C : I'd _____ the shrimp platter.

B : And what would you like to _____ ?

A : Can you show us the _____ list ?

B : _____ , sir.

(2) **Cartoon**

Lesson 11

I Don't Feel Very Well

Listen and repeat
after your teacher.

🎧 (A) LET'S TALK

A : Are you all right?

B : I don't feel very well.

A : You look pale. What's wrong?

B : My nose is stopped up, and I have a headache.

A : Maybe you're coming down with something.

B : I hear there's a bug going around.

A : Do you want me to make a doctor's appointment
for you?

B : I guess I can wait for my annual check-up.

A : You ought to stay in bed and drink plenty of liquids.

B : I'm probably just run-down and need a rest.

LESSON 11

● (B) LET'S PRACTICE

Learn the following phrases and do the practice with your partner.

(1) **Not Feeling Well**

1. You look pale.
2. You have no energy.
3. Is anything wrong with you?

4. I'm not feeling well.
5. I feel dizzy.
6. I am allergic to cat hair.

(2) **Aches and Pains**

7. My body aches all over.
8. I have a splitting headache.
9. I have a sore throat.
10. I have a fever.
11. I've caught a cold.
12. I cough severely.

13. I have a ringing in my ears.
14. I have a toothache.
15. I have a pain in the shoulder.

PRACTICE 1

Work in pairs. Take turns asking each other "What's wrong with you?" and answering according to the situations below.

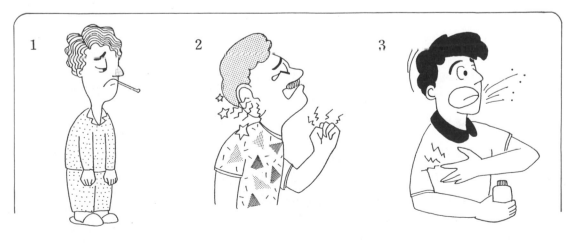

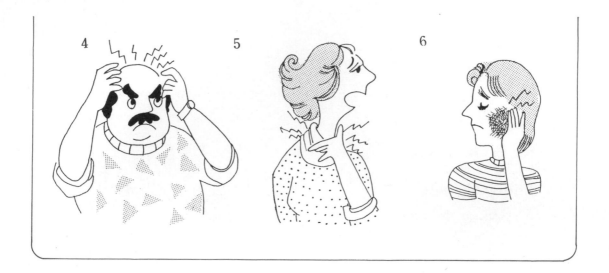

(3) Stomach Upsets

16. I have no appetite.
17. I have indigestion.
18. I have loose bowels.
19. I'm constipated.

20. I have diarrhea.
21. I have a stomachache.
22. I feel like vomitting.

(4) Injuries

23. I'm afraid I have a broken leg.
24. I have a sprained ankle.

25. I am bleeding heavily.
26. I burned my hand.
27. I got hurt in the arm.

(5) Doctor's Orders

28. Will I have to stay in bed ?
29. You'd better lie in bed for a while.
30. You better rest a little.
31. Do I need stitches ?
32. Can you give me something for it ?
33. How often do I take this ?

34. Could you have a look at it for me?

35. Please tell me how to take the medicine.

36. Is it all right to eat anything?

37. Do I have to be operated on?

PRACTICE 2

Work in pairs. One of you is a doctor, and the other is sick or hurt in the ways below. The patient should say what is wrong, the doctor should prescribe a treatment.

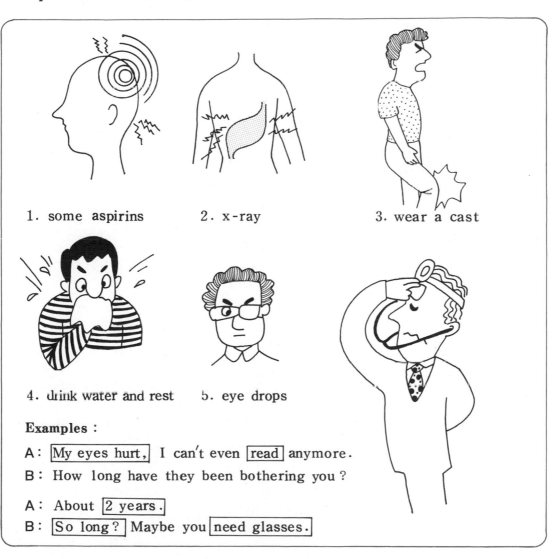

1. some aspirins   2. x-ray   3. wear a cast

4. drink water and rest   5. eye drops

Examples:

A: My eyes hurt, I can't even read anymore.

B: How long have they been bothering you?

A: About 2 years.

B: So long? Maybe you need glasses.

LESSON 11

🎧 (C) LET'S PLAY
● For Student A

Learn the following sentence patterns first, and ask your partner for the information you need.

What How	do you think	about of	this combination ? Paul and Clara ?

I think Maybe It could be that	they John and Judith	would wouldn't	make a good couple, get along well together,

because	they both both of them	like	to read. rock-n-roll.
	Paul is too old for Clara. they have different hobbies.		

● **You work for a matchmaking service. Your partner has a list of three available women. Ask for their information first, then decide which combination would be the most compatible.**

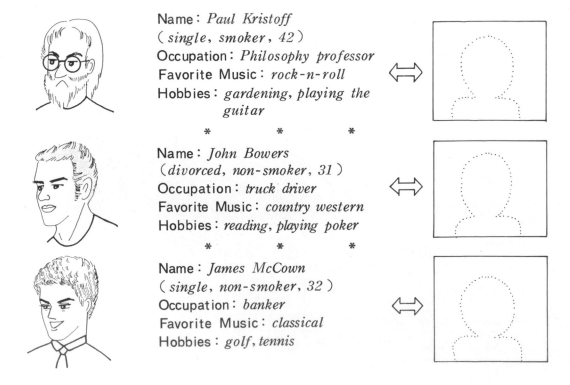

Name : *Paul Kristoff*
(*single, smoker, 42*)
Occupation : *Philosophy professor*
Favorite Music : *rock-n-roll*
Hobbies : *gardening, playing the guitar*

*   *   *

Name : *John Bowers*
(*divorced, non-smoker, 31*)
Occupation : *truck driver*
Favorite Music : *country western*
Hobbies : *reading, playing poker*

*   *   *

Name : *James McCown*
(*single, non-smoker, 32*)
Occupation : *banker*
Favorite Music : *classical*
Hobbies : *golf, tennis*

LESSON 11

(C) LET'S PLAY

• For Student B

Learn the following sentence patterns first, and ask your partner for the information you need.

What How	do you think	of about	this combination ? Paul and Clara ?

I think Maybe It could be that	they John and Judith	would wouldn't	make a good couple, get along well together,

because	they both both of them	like	to read. rock-n-roll.
	Paul is too old for Clara. they have different hobbies.		

• **You work for a matchmaking service. Your partner has a list of three available men. Ask for their information first, then decide which combination would be the most compatible.**

Name: *Diana Smith*
(*divorced, smoker, 26*)
Occupation: *waitress*
Favorite Music: *rock-n-roll*
Hobbies: *astrology, meditation*

*　　　*　　　*

Name: *Clara Jones*
(*single, non-smoker, 24*)
Occupation: *writer*
Favorite Music: *classical*
Hobbies: *dog breeding, computers*

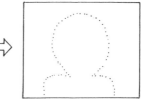

*　　　*　　　*

Name: *Judith Wayne*
(*divorced, two children, non-smoker, 30*)
Occupation: *teacher*
Favorite Music: *jazz*
Hobbies: *raising money for charity*

LESSON 11

Exercise

Complete the following dialogue and make your own conversation.

(1) **Dialogue**

A : How are you getting on ?

B : _____ .

A : Oh, really ? What's the matter ?

B : _____ .

A : That's too bad.

　　　*　　　*　　　*　　　*　　　*

A : Good morning. _____?

B : I've had a pretty _____ since yesterday morning.

A : Anything else ?

B : Yes, I have _____ .

A : I see. We'll take a good ____ at you.

(2) **Cartoon**

Lesson 12 I'm Looking for a Pair of Shoes

Listen and repeat
after your teacher.

(A) LET'S TALK

A : Good morning, sir. Can I help you?
B : Yes, I'm looking for a pair of shoes.

A : Okay. What size do you wear?
B : Size 10.

A : Any particular color?
B : I like black.

A : How about this pair?
B : No, I don't think so.

A : How about these?
B : I like this pair. Mind if I try them on?

A : Go right ahead.
B : Hey! They fit perfectly!

🎧 (B) LET'S PRACTICE

Learn the following phrases and do the practice with your partner.

(1) In the Store

1. What are your hours?
2. Where is the duty-free shop?
3. Is there a souvenir shop near here?
4. What time does this store open?
5. May I help you?
6. What can I do for you?
7. On which floor can I buy sporting goods?

(2) I'm Looking for ⋯

8. I'm just looking. Thanks.
9. I'd like to look around some more.
10. I want to buy a pair of shoes.
11. I'd like to see some bookcases.
12. I want a new battery for my watch. Which floor should I go to?
13. I'm looking for a shirt to match these trousers.
14. I want to return this. Is that possible?
15. Will you give me a refund?

PRACTICE I

Work in pairs. Take turns asking "May I help you?" Answer as follows:

1. just looking

2. return a broken watch

3. looking for a shirt

4. get to know the open hours

5. where to buy toys

(3) Examining the Merchandise

16. What karat gold is this?

17. What's this stone?

18. Where was this made?

19. What material is this made of?

20. Is this washable?

21. I'd like to try this on, please.

22. Where is the fitting room?

23. This doesn't fit me.

24. The arms are too short.

25. It's a little loose around the waist.

26. This is a little too large.

27. Have you got this in other sizes?

28. Do you have a cheaper one in the same style?

29. I'm afraid it's not quite what I was looking for. I think I'll leave it.

(4) Second Thoughts

30. How much is it?

31. How much does it cost?
32. What's the price?
33. Is this merchandise guaranteed?
34. Can you give me a discount?
35. Can you make the price lower?
36. Can't you make it cheaper?
37. I'll take it.
38. I'll take this one.

PRACTICE 2

Work in pairs. Take turns practicing conversation between the shopper and clerk. Use the situations below.

1. It's too big.

2. You don't like the color.

3. You want a warranty.

4. You only have 200 N.T.

5. You want to try on this silk dress and find out where it was made.

6. Do your best to persuade your customer to buy the Citizen Watch instead of the CASIO Watch.

PRACTICE 3

Work in pairs. Practice saying these prices. Use this model:

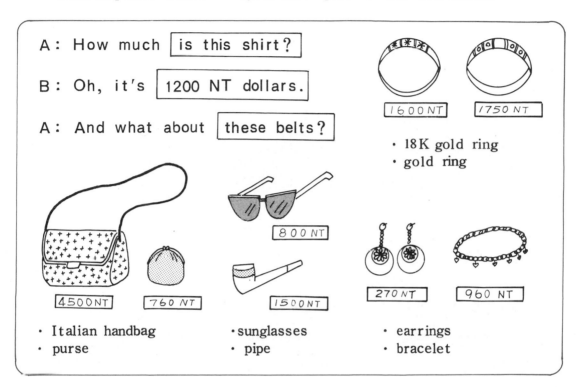

A: How much │is this shirt?│

B: Oh, it's │1200 NT dollars.│

A: And what about │these belts?│

│1600NT│ │1750 NT│

· 18K gold ring
· gold ring

│4500NT│ │760 NT│ │1500NT│ │800 NT│ │270 NT│ │960 NT│

· Italian handbag
· purse

·sunglasses
· pipe

· earrings
· bracelet

LESSON 12

🎧 (C) LET'S PLAY

• For the Whole Class

Learn the following sentence patterns first, and do the following role-play.

I'm looking for a pair of	shoes.
	sneakers.
Do you have any	size ten?

What	kind	do you want?
	size	
Here you are.		

Sorry, we	don't have any	cowboy boots.
	are out of	size ten.

Thanks anyway.

How much are they?
What's the price?

I'll take them.
I think I'll look around some more.

● **Buying & Selling shoes — directions for the teacher**

1. Divide your students into two teams: shoppers and clerks.

2. Let the shoppers choose one shoe size from among the shoe sizes below.

6	7	8	9	10

3. Every shopper writes down his shoe size on 8 pieces of paper. The teacher collects those pieces of paper and let the clerks draw lots from them.

4. Every clerk must have 8 pieces of paper. These are the sizes for the 8 pairs of shoes in their shop.

5. Every clerk should write down his name, the style of shoes, and the price on each slip.

   Example :

John **Cowboy boots** size : 8 price : US $ 15

6. Let the students read the role cards, then begin.

SHOPPERS

Each of you has US$100 to spend on shoes. Buy as many pairs as you can, but only in your shoe size! Write down the price of every pair you buy, and shop around for bargains.

CLERKS

Each of you has paid US$100 for eight pairs of shoes, in the styles shown below. Mark the price for each pair. Make as much money as you can by selling them to shoppers. (Remember — you cannot sell any pair more than once.)

cowboy boots
size _____
price _____

combat boots
size _____
price _____

sneakers
size _____
price _____

high heels
size _____
price _____

sandals
size _____
price _____

loafers
size _____
price _____

bedroom slippers
size _____
price _____

pirate boots
size _____
price _____

- How many pairs of shoes did you buy?
- Which clerk earned the most money?

LESSON 12

Exercise

Complete the following dialogue and make your own conversation.

(1) **Dialogue**

A : _____ , sir?

B : _____ . Will you show me some gold chains?

A : Certainly, sir. We have a large selection of gold chains. All of them are in the two-hundred-dollar price range.

B : _____ ?

A : This one?

B : Yes.

A : _____ . It's fourteen-karat gold.

B : Really? Yes, it's very nice, but _____ .

A : This one's the same style, but it's shorter.

B : Yes, that's what I'm _____ . _____ .

(2) **Cartoon**

① _____ , where's the _____ ?

② It's on this floor, and just over there.

① This is a little too big. Do you _____ ?

② Sure.

Lesson 13 I'd Like to Send This Package

Listen and repeat
after your teacher.

(A) LET'S TALK

A : I'd like to send this package to Taiwan.
B : What does it contain?

A : It contains clothes.
B : Do you want it registered?

A : Yes, please. How much will it be?
B : Ten dollars.

A : Then, give me three twenty-cent stamps. By the way, how long does it take?
B : Here you are. It takes five days.

LESSON 13

🎧 (B) LET'S PRACTICE

Learn the following phrases and do the practice with your partner.

(1) Sending Letters

1. Will you mail this letter for me?

2. I'd like to send these letters to Taiwan by air mail.

3. I'.d like to send this by special delivery.

4. Please send it by registered mail.

5. I'd like to send this as printed matter.

6. What's the registration fee?

7. How many days does it take to reach Taiwan by sea mail?

(2) Buying Stamps, Postcards and Aerograms

8. Where can I get postage stamps?

9. How much is the postage?

10. I'd like to have five postcards.

11. May I have ten aerograms, please?

12. Please give me three twenty-cent stamps.

13. Do you have any commemorative stamps?

14. How much should I pay for this?

15. How much is it altogether?

(3) Mailing a Package

16. Will you weigh this package for me?

17. Is that within the weight limit?

18. What's in this package?

19. What does it contain?

PRACTICE 1

Work in pairs. You and your partner take turns playing a postal employee and a person going to the post office.

1. You'd like to send two registered letters by air mail to New York. You want to know how much is the postage.

2. You want to buy 10 postcards, 5 twenty-cent stamps and 2 aerograms.

3. You want to mail 10 letters as printed matter, and want to know how long the delivery takes.

4. You'd like to send a package of books by airmail and want to know if it is within the weight limit.

(4) **At the Bank**

20. Could you cash a traveler's check for 100 dollars?

21. Could you break this into small change?

22. Could you break this 100 dollar bill?

23. How would you like your money?

24. I'd like 5 ten-dollar bills, 3 five dollar bills and the rest in small change.

25. Will you change NT dollars into American dollars?

26. What's the exchange rate for NT dollars today?

27. I'd like to open an account.

28. I'd like to deposit 100 dollars.

29. I would like to deposit some money in the bank.

30. Do you have any identification?

31. Please endorse your check.

PRACTICE 2

Work in pairs. One of you is the clerk at the bank, the other is the customer. The customer should request for the following services, and the clerk should react accordingly. Then switch roles.

The customer wants...

1. to change 2600 N.T. dollars into U.S. dollars

2. to learn the exchange rate for today (26)

3. 8 ten-dollar bills and 20 one-dollar bills

4. to cash a traveler's check for 150 U.S. dollars

5. one one-hundred-dollar bill and 10 five-dollar bills

6. to deposit 100 U.S. dollars in your account (you are asked to fill up a deposit slip)

LESSON 13

🔈 (C) LET'S PLAY

● Work in Pairs

Learn the following sentence patterns first, and ask your partner for the information you need.

Are	you	an introvert?
Do		tend to be introverted?

No,	I	am an extrovert.
Yes,		tend to be introverted.

I	make decisions	based on	reason.
	decide things		emotion.
			intuition.

My life	is changing.
	stays the same.
I'm going through a lot of changes.	

What	is your sign?	I'm	a Gemini.
	sign are you?		an Aries.

PERSONAL INFORMATION

● STEP 1

Find your western astrological sign using the chart below. This represents what sign of the zodiac the sun was in when you were born.

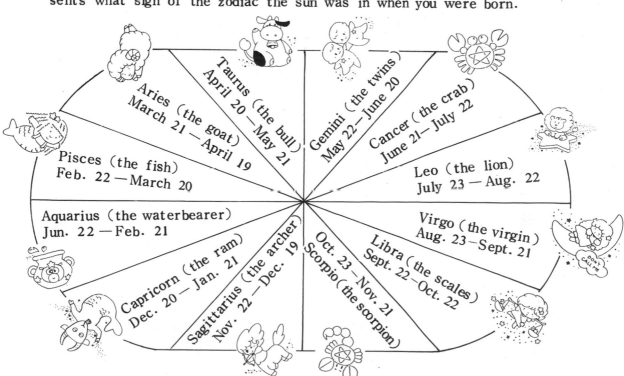

Aries (the goat)
March 21 — April 19

Taurus (the bull)
April 20 — May 21

Gemini (the twins)
May 22 — June 20

Cancer (the crab)
June 21 — July 22

Leo (the lion)
July 23 — Aug. 22

Virgo (the virgin)
Aug. 23 — Sept. 21

Libra (the scales)
Sept. 22 — Oct. 22

Scorpio (the scorpion)
Oct. 23 — Nov. 21

Sagittarius (the archer)
Nov. 22 — Dec. 19

Capricorn (the ram)
Dec. 20 — Jan. 21

Aquarius (the waterbearer)
Jun. 22 — Feb. 21

Pisces (the fish)
Feb. 22 — March 20

● STEP 2

Find your partner's astrological sign by asking the following questions:

1	Are you an introvert or an extrovert?

Extrovert	Introvert
Aries	Taurus
Gemini	Cancer
Leo	Virgo
Libra	Capricorn
Sagittarius	Pisces
Aquarius	

2	Does your life move forward, stay the same or just change a lot?

Forward	Same	Change
Aries	Taurus	Gemini
Cancer	Leo	Virgo
Libra	Scorpio	Sagittarius
Capricorn	Aquarius	Pisces

3	Do you make decisions based on emotion, practicality, reason or intuition?

Emotion	Practicality
Aries	Taurus
Leo	Virgo
Sagittarius	Capricorn

Reason	Intuition
Gemini	Cancer
Libra	Scorpio
Aquarius	Pisces

> For example, if you are an introverted, intuitive person whose life is generally moving forward, you would probably like the sign of Cancer. Why? Because Cancer appears under all three lists for your answers!

● **Now, check to see if this sign matches your partner's sign!**

● STEP 3

Here are some more words related to 12 astrological signs. Tell your partner about his(her) sign and see if that matches his(her) personality.

Aries: ambitious
purposeful
headstrong
self-reliant
imaginative
Examples:
  Charlie Chaplin
  Vincent Van Gogh
	Taurus: practical
	solid
	stubborn
	strong-willed
	conservative
	Examples:
	  Catherine the Great
	  Oliver Cromwell
		Gemini: multi-sided
		changable
		self-controlled
		restless
		complex
		Examples:
		  John F. Kennedy
		  Marilyn Monroe

Cancer: passive
clinging
nurturing
mystical
home-loving
Examples:
  Ernest Hemingway
  Rembrandt
	Leo: proud
	masterful
	confident
	dominating
	natural leader
	Examples:
	  Benito Mussolini
	  Napoleon Bonaparte
		Virgo: methodical
		reserved
		nervous
		orderly
		exacting
		DON'T CALL ME
		Examples:
		  Queen Elizabeth I
		  Cardinal Richelieu

Libra: balanced
good judgement
harmonious
elegant
impartial
Examples:
  Mohandas Gandhi
  Brigette Bardot
	Scorpio: treacherous
	manipulative
	hypnotic
	powerful
	emotional
	Examples:
	  Katherine Hepburn
	  Marie Curie
		Sagittarius: honest
		optimistic
		independent
		outspoken
		initiative
		Examples:
		  Winston Churchill

Capricorn: complaining
cautious
suspicious
melancholy
shrewd
Examples:
  Sir Isaac Newton
  Benjamin Franklin
	Aquarius: refined
	aristocratic
	forceful
	sincere
	idealistic
	Examples:
	  Charles Darwin
	  Ronald Reagan
		Pisces: subtle
		sympathetic
		romantic
		patient
		sensitive
		Examples:
		  George Washington
		  Elizabeth Taylor

LESSON 13

Exercise

Complete the following dialogue and make your own conversation.

(1) Dialogue

A : Will you please _____ for me?

B : Certainly. Please endorse it first.   Do you _____ _____ ?

A : Yes, I do. Here is my driver's license.

B : Thank you. _____ ?

A : Please give me 7 ten dollar bills and 6 five dollar bills.

B : _____.   Please check to see that you have the right amount.

(2) Cartoon

Lesson 14 Review

🎧 (A) LET'S WRITE

Fill in the blanks and make your own conversation.

1

A : _, I'm David Lee.

B : _____ you. I'm Jane White.

A : _____ a drink?

B : Yes, please.

A : What _____, Jane?

B : I work for _____ .

2

A : _____ with you?

B : About the same. _____?

A : So-so, I guess.

B : Listen, how would you like _____ next Saturday?

A : I'd love to!

3

A : Excuse me. May I _____ ?

B : Of course, if it's anything _____.

A : _____ to take our picture with this camera?

B : Sure.

A : Thank you_____ your help.

B : You are _____.

4

A : _____where today's paper is?

B : I saw it in _____.

A : Sorry_____ you, but would you go and bring it for me?

B : _____. Here it is.

A : _____ .

5

A : _____ tomorrow afternoon?

B : Yes, I think so.

A : Then how about _____ ?

B : _____. At what time?

A : Is two o'clock too early?

B : No,_____.

6

A : _____, but is that Professor Smith's office?

B : Huh?   I _____ ?

A : I'm looking   Professor Smith!

B : Oh, that's_____ I thought you said.

A : I don't follow you. _____ ?

B : Sorry.... you see, I'm Professor Smith.

7

A: Are you looking _____ to your new job?

B: Yeah, I guess so.

A: Well, I'm sure _____ .

B: I've been applying ___ graduate schools, Uncle Bob.

A: _____! I always knew you were a scholar.

B: I hope _____ .

8

A: Oh, I'm sorry for _____ . Have I kept you waiting long?

B: No, you haven't. I also come _____ .

A: I'm glad _____ . The traffic was so heavy.

B: Yes, I know. It's _____

_____ .

9

A: Here is _____ for you.

B: Oh, thank you very much! _____ open it now?

A: Sure, _____ .

B: Oh, what a lovely blouse! Thank you.

A: I hope _____

10

B: _____ to order?

A: Yes, I believe I'll have a steak _____ that lady's
having.

B: And _____ cooked?

A : Medium rare. Do I get salad with that?

B : Yes, and _____ to drink?

A : I'll have a martini.

B : Very good, sir. _____ .

11

A : You look ____. What's _____?

B : My nose is stopped up, and _____ a headache.

A : Maybe you're _____ something.

B : I hear there's a____going around.

A : You ought to _____and _____

12

A : Good morning, sir._____ ?

B : Yes, _____ a pair of shoes.

A : Okay. _____do you wear?

B : Size 10.

A : _____ this pair?

B : I like this pair._____ I try them on?

A : Go right ahead.

13

A : _____ send this package to Taiwan.

B : _____ ?

A : It contains clothes.

B : Do you want it registered?

A : Yes, please. _____ ?

B : Ten dollars.

A: By the way, _____ ?

B: It takes five days.

LESSON 14

🎧 (B) LET'S PLAY

Read the following direction and do the roleplay.

1. Work in a group of three. Decide who will be A, B and C.

2. Each of you reads the activity card for your own part only.   No peeking!

3. When you finish Activity 1, go on to Activity 2, and so on.

4. If you like, you can perform the skit again for the whole class.

ROLE CARDS

ROLE ACTIVITY CARDS [1]

A
You are hosting a cocktail party. When the doorbell rings, go welcome your guest C.

B
You were invited to this party and have already arrived.

C
You are on your way to the party. Now you are about to ring the doorbell.

A₁
Answer the door, and introduce B and C.

B₁
Wait for A to introduce you to C and react to the situation.

C₁
Enter and apologize for being late.

A₂
Offer B and C something to drink.

B₂
You've heard that C just graduated from Yale University. Say something to C.

C₂
React to the situation.

A₃
You ask B about his(her) brother.

B₃
Your brother just caught a bad cold last night, but feels better today.

C₃
You are distracted by a young lady passing by, so you don't hear B's words clearly. Ask B to repeat.

Now it's time to leave.

A₄
React to B and C.

B₄
Mention how late it is. Thank A for inviting you.

C₄
Thank A. Suggest having him over to your house sometime.

Good Bye !

ROLE CARDS ②

ROLE CARDS

A
You and B are at the shopping mall.

B
You and A are at the shopping mall.

C
You are the clerk at each store.

ROLE ACTIVITY CARDS

A₁
You are looking for a small blue sweater.

B₁
You think A should try them on.

C₁
You have small green sweaters and large blue sweaters. Try to persuade A to buy the green one.

A₂
Ask the prices of the sweaters and decide on one.

B₂
You want A to make sure the goods come with a guarantee.

C₂
React to the situation.

A₃
You and B go to the post office. You withdraw money here.

B₃
You want to send a package through the mail.

C₃
A needs to fill in the withdrawal slip. B needs a customs declaration, insurance form, and $30.00 worth of stamps.

It's time to eat!

A₄
You would like an English menu. You are a vegetarian, but eggs and milk are okay.

B₄
You would like the table by the window.

C₄
Seat A and B first. Then give A an English menu. Make some suggestions for A. Take A and B's order.

Enjoy your meal!

Boys' Names For You

Alan〔ˈælən〕亞倫
Albert〔ˈælbət〕艾伯特
Andrew〔ˈændru〕安德魯
Andy〔ˈændɪ〕安廸
Antony〔ˈæntənɪ〕安東尼
Arthur〔ˈɑrθɚ〕亞瑟
Bert〔bɝt〕伯特
Bill〔bɪl〕比爾
Bob〔bɑb〕鮑伯
Brian〔ˈbraɪən〕布萊恩
Bruce〔brus〕布魯斯
Carl〔kɑrl〕卡爾
Charles〔tʃɑrlz〕查爾斯
Christopher〔ˈkrɪstəfɚ〕克里斯多夫
Clement〔ˈklɛmənt〕克萊曼
Colin〔kɑlin〕科林
Cyril〔ˈsɪrəl〕西瑞爾
Daniel〔ˈdænɪəl〕丹尼爾
David〔ˈdevɪd〕大衞
Dean〔din〕廸恩
Dennis〔ˈdɛnɪs〕丹尼斯
Dick〔dɪk〕狄克
Donald〔ˈdɑnl̩d〕唐納德
Douglas〔ˈdʌgləs〕道格拉斯
Edwin〔ˈɛdwɪn〕愛德溫
Edmund〔ˈɛdmənd〕艾德蒙
Edward〔ˈɛdwɚd〕艾德華
Eric〔ˈɛrɪk〕艾立克
Eugene〔juˈdʒin〕尤金
Felix〔ˈfilɪks〕菲力克斯
Fred〔frɛd〕弗瑞德
Frank〔fræŋk〕法蘭克
Gary〔ˈgɛrɪ〕蓋里
Geoffrey〔ˈdʒɛfrɪ〕傑弗瑞
George〔dʒɔrdʒ〕喬治
Harry〔ˈhærɪ〕哈利
Henry〔ˈhɛnrɪ〕亨利
Jack〔dʒæk〕傑克

James〔dʒemz〕詹姆斯
Jim〔dʒɪm〕吉姆
Joe〔dʒo〕喬
John〔dʒɑn〕約翰
Joseph〔ˈdʒozəf〕約瑟夫
Ken〔kɛn〕肯恩
Kevin〔ˈkɛvɪn〕凱文
Larry〔ˈlærɪ〕賴利
Lawrence〔ˈlɔrəns〕勞倫斯
Louis〔ˈlʊɪs〕路易斯
Mark〔mɑrk〕馬克
Michael〔ˈmaɪkl̩〕麥克
Neil〔nil〕尼爾
Oliver〔ˈɑləvɚ〕奧立弗
Patrick〔ˈpætrɪk〕派區克
Paul〔pɔl〕保羅
Peter〔ˈpitɚ〕彼得
Philip〔ˈfɪləp〕菲力浦
Ralph〔rælf〕雷爾夫
Ray〔re〕雷伊
Raymond〔ˈremənd〕雷蒙德
Richard〔ˈrɪtʃɚd〕理查
Robert〔ˈrɑbɚt〕羅伯特
Robin〔ˈrɑbɪn〕羅賓
Roger〔ˈrɑdʒɚ〕羅吉
Sam〔sæm〕山姆
Simon〔ˈsaɪmən〕賽門
Stanley〔ˈstænlɪ〕史丹利
Stephen〔ˈstivən〕史蒂芬
Stuart〔ˈstjuɚt〕史都華
Sydney〔ˈsɪdnɪ〕錫德尼
Ted〔tɛd〕泰德
Thomas〔ˈtɑməs〕湯瑪斯
Timothy〔ˈtɪməθɪ〕提摩西
Tony〔ˈtonɪ〕東尼
Victor〔ˈvɪktɚ〕維克多
William〔ˈwɪljəm〕威廉

Girls' Names For You

Agatha〔'ægəθə〕愛嘉莎	Joyce〔dʒɔɪs〕喬伊絲
Alice〔'ælɪs〕愛麗絲	Judy〔'dʒudɪ〕朱蒂
Amanda〔ə'mændə〕艾曼塔	Julia〔'dʒuljə〕朱麗亞
Amy〔'emɪ〕艾美	Kitty〔'kɪtɪ〕吉蒂
Angela〔'ændʒələ〕安琪拉	Laura〔'lɔrə〕羅拉
Anita〔ə'nitə〕艾妮塔	Linda〔'lɪndə〕琳達
Ann〔æn〕安	Lucy〔'lusɪ〕露西
Audrey〔'ɔdrɪ〕奧黛莉	Maggie〔'mægɪ〕瑪姬
Barbara〔'bɑrbərə〕芭芭拉	Margaret〔'mɑrgrɪt〕瑪格麗特
Betty〔'bɛtɪ〕貝蒂	Maria〔mə'rɪə〕瑪麗亞
Catherine〔'kæθərɪn〕凱薩琳	Marilyn〔'mærəlɪn〕瑪洛琳
Christine〔krɪs'tin〕克莉絲汀	Martha〔'mɑrθə〕瑪莎
Daisy〔'dezɪ〕黛西	Mary〔'mɛrɪ〕瑪莉
Daphne〔'dæfnɪ〕黛芙妮	May〔me〕玫
Deborah〔'dɛbərə〕黛博拉	Molly〔'mɑlɪ〕茉莉
Denise〔də'niz〕丹妮絲	Monica〔'mɑnɪkə〕茉妮卡
Diana〔daɪ'ænə〕黛安娜	Nancy〔'nænsɪ〕南茜
Doris〔'dɔrɪs〕桃麗絲	Natalie〔'nætl̩ɪ〕娜特莉
Elizabeth〔ɪ'lɪzəbəθ〕伊麗沙白	Olivia〔o'lɪvɪə〕奧莉薇亞
Emily〔'ɛml̩ɪ〕艾美莉	Paula〔'pɔlə〕珀拉
Emma〔'ɛmə〕艾瑪	Phoebe〔'fibɪ〕菲碧
Evelyn〔'ivlɪn〕伊芙琳	Rebecca〔rɪ'bɛkə〕麗蓓嘉
Fanny〔'fænɪ〕芬妮	Rita〔'ritə〕麗達
Fiona〔fɪ'onə〕費歐娜	Rose〔roz〕羅絲
Flora〔'flɔrə〕芙蘿拉	Sally〔'sælɪ〕莎莉
Frances〔'frænsɪs〕法蘭西絲	Samantha〔sə'mænθə〕莎曼莎
Gloria〔'glorɪə〕葛蘿莉亞	Sandra〔'sændrə〕桑德拉
Grace〔gres〕葛莉斯	Sarah〔'sɛrə〕莎拉
Helen〔'hɛlən〕海倫	Shirley〔'ʃɜlɪ〕雪莉
Isabella〔ˌɪzə'bɛlə〕伊莎蓓拉	Sonia〔'sonɪə〕蘇妮亞
Jacqueline〔'dʒækəlɪn〕賈桂琳	Sophia〔sə'faɪə, 'sofɪə〕蘇菲亞
Jane〔dʒen〕珍	Stella〔'stɛlə〕史黛拉
Janet〔'dʒænɪt〕珍尼特	Susan〔'suzn̩〕蘇珊
Jennifer〔'dʒɛnəfə〕珍尼弗	Teresa〔tə'risə〕泰莉莎
Jessica〔'dʒɛsəkə〕傑西嘉	Tina〔'tinə〕提娜
Jill〔dʒɪl〕吉兒	Tracy〔'tresɪ〕崔西
Joan〔dʒon〕瓊	Victoria〔vɪk'torɪə〕維多莉亞
Josephine〔'dʒozə,fin〕約瑟芬	

||||||||||||| ●學習出版公司門市部● |||||||||||||||

台北地區：台北市許昌街 10 號 2 樓 TEL：(02)2331-4060・2331-9209
台中地區：台中市綠川東街 32 號 8 樓 23 室
　　　　　TEL：(04)2223-2838

|||||||||||||||||||||||||||||||||||||||||||||

ALL　TALKS ①

編　　著 / 陳 怡 平
發 行 所 / 學習出版有限公司　　　　　☎ (02) 2704-5525
郵 撥 帳 號 / 0512727-2 學習出版社帳戶
登 記 證 / 局版台業 *2179* 號
印 刷 所 / 紅藍彩藝印刷股份有限公司
台 北 門 市 / 台北市許昌街 10 號 2 F　　☎ (02) 2331-4060・2331-9209
台 中 門 市 / 台中市綠川東街 32 號 8 F 23 室　☎ (04) 2223-2838
台灣總經銷 / 紅螞蟻圖書有限公司　　　☎ (02) 2799-9490・2657-0132
美國總經銷 / Evergreen　Book　Store　☎ (818) 2813622

售價：新台幣一百八十元正
2002 年 1 月 1 日一版四刷

ISBN 957-519-198-6

第 一 冊 學 習 內 容 一 覽 表

LESSON	CONVERSATION	TYPICAL PHRASES	ACTIVITY	EXERCISE
1	Nice to Meet You	初次與人見面時的應對語句，如招呼問候、自我介紹、詢問工作職業等。	兩人一組的活動，練習用簡易的句型，互相問答某人從哪裡來，工作年齡、婚姻狀況等基本個人資料。	Complete Dialogues
2	See You Next Week	遇到熟人時的招呼用語，及各種道別的實用例句，包括代問候他人及表示即將離開的用語。	全班一起參與的活動。互相問答，練習各種簡易的過去式及現在式的基本句型。	Complete Dialogues
3	Thank You for Your Help	要求他人幫忙的用語，及各種表示願意協助、感謝對方時的實況例句。	活動1：兩人一組的活動。練習如何描述他人的外貌。 活動2：全班一起參與，練習描述自己班上的同學。	Complete Dialogues
4	Would You Please Open the Window?	如何用英文要求他人、徵求允許及提出建議等的語句。包括表同意或拒絕時的應對例句。	兩人一組的活動。練習用英文向對方借東西。	Complete Dialogues
5	How about a Game of Tennis?	有關用英文陳述建議的例句，包括徵詢建議、提出建議、及表示接受或否絕提議的用語。	兩人一組的角色扮演，討論假期中要做什麼活動。輪流提出建議及徵求建議。	Complete Dialogues
6	I Beg Your Pardon	各種表示沒聽清楚，要求重覆一次時的用語。	兩人一組的對答活動。練習可數名詞和不可數名詞的說法。	Complete Dialogues
7	Congratulations	包括用英文讚美對方，回謝對方讚美、恭賀他人、回敬他人的道賀、及各式節日祝福語的實用例句。	活動1：全班一起來玩「比手劃腳」，用英文問問題及說出答案。 活動2：兩人一組，看圖說故事。練習 There is/are～，現在進行式及 because 的句型。	Complete Dialogues
8	I'm Sorry for Being Late	練習用英文道歉，接受道歉，及慰問他人的實用語句。	兩人一組的活動，練習詢問某事是否被允許的句型。	Complete Dialogues
9	That's Great	各種表達情緒的用語，包括高興、悲傷、忿怒、驚訝等。	兩人一組的對話活動。練習表推測語氣的句型。	Complete Dialogues
10	I'll Have a Steak	各種在西餐廳點餐、用餐及付帳時的實用語句。	兩人一組的角色扮演。輪流當侍者及顧客，練習用英文在西餐廳點菜。	Complete Dialogues
11	I Don't Feel Very Well	各種身體病痛的表達法，如牙痛、胃痛、頭痛等。及看醫生時的實況例句。	兩人一組的活動。充當紅娘，練習為三組新人配對。 詢問及表達看法的句型。	Complete Dialogues
12	I'm Looking for a Pair of Shoes	練習各種購物的實用語句，從比較挑選、詢問價格、討價還價到成交付款實況等。	活動1：全班一起參與的活動。輪流當店員與顧客，看哪一組的生意最好。	Complete Dialogues
13	I'd Like to Send This Package	到郵局去寄信、寄包裹及到銀行存、提款等的實用語句。	兩人一組的活動。用英文為同伴分析個性及星座占卜。	Complete Dialogues
14	Review	填充題：複習 1-13 課的會話（ conversation ）。	角色扮演：三個人一組的活動，複習 1-13 課所學內容。	

EUR

The Valley of the
Kings, Egypt

Majorca, Spain（馬約卡島）

Villandry Castle, France

The Ginkakuji Temple, Japan（銀閣寺）

San Francisco Bay